ARTHUR'S NOSE

by

Marc Brown

Little, Brown and Company
BOSTON   TORONTO   LONDON

BOOKS ILLUSTRATED BY MARC BROWN

The Iron Lion

I Found It in the Yellow Pages

Four Corners of the Sky

HC: 10 9 8 7 6 5

PB: 10 9 8 7 6 5

Library of Congress Cataloging in Publication Data

Brown, Marc Tolon.
  Arthur's nose.

  SUMMARY: Unhappy with his nose, Arthur visits the rhinologist to get a new one.

  [1. Nose — Fiction. 2. Animals — Fiction]
I. Title
PZ7.B81618Ar   [E]   75-30610
ISBN 0-316-11070-1 pbk.

Joy Street Books are published
by Little, Brown and Company (Inc.)

WOR

Published simultaneously in Canada
by Little, Brown & Company (Canada) Limited

PRINTED IN THE UNITED STATES OF AMERICA

This is Arthur's house.

This is Arthur.
He is worried
about his nose.

This is Arthur's mom.

This is Arthur's dad.

This is Arthur's sister.

They all love Arthur, and they all like his nose.

One day Arthur decided he didn't like his nose.
He had a cold and his nose was red.
His sister thought his nose looked funny.

His nose was a nuisance at school.
Francine, who sat in front of Arthur, complained to the
teacher that Arthur's nose was always bothering her.

When Arthur played hide-and-seek,
friends always found him first.

His friends thought his nose was funny.
But what could he do about it?

He could change his nose!
That's what he could
do about it.

Arthur told his friends that he was going
to the rhinologist for a new nose.
His friends were very surprised.

Doctor Louise was very helpful. She suggested that Arthur try on pictures of different noses. That way he could choose the one he liked best.

Arthur tried on all kinds of noses.

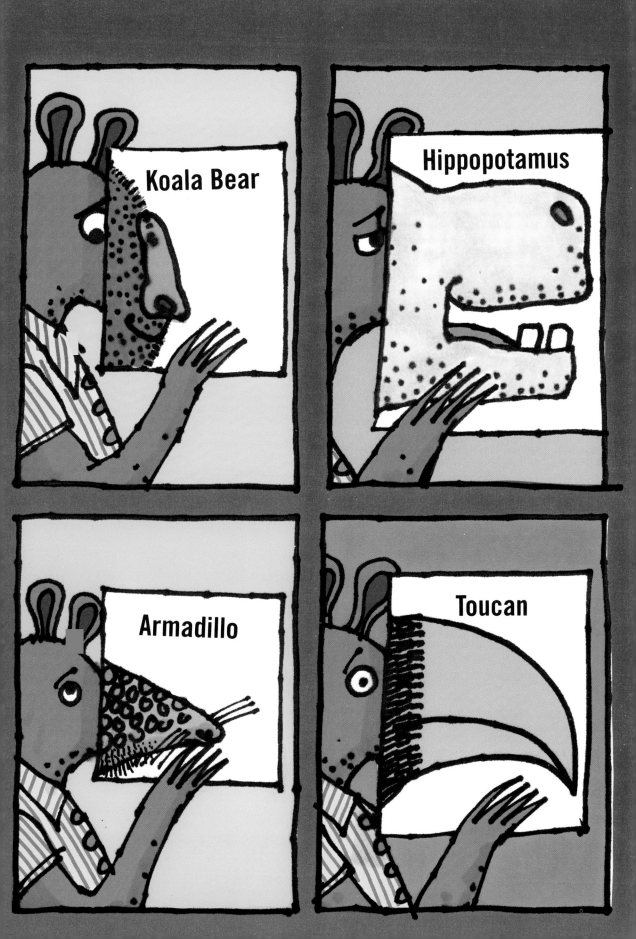

This was going to be a difficult decision.

Arthur hadn't changed his nose at all.

"I tried on every nose there was.
I'm just not me without my nose!"
said Arthur.

It's a nice nose.

There's a lot more to Arthur than his nose.

Ms. Yollanda
Grade 1